2005

Enrico
Starts School

For my mum and dad

First published in the United States by
Dial Books for Young Readers
A division of Penguin Young Readers Group
345 Hudson Street
New York, New York 10014
Published in the United Kingdom
by Gullane Children's Books
Copyright © 2004 by Charlotte Middleton
All rights reserved
Manufactured in China
1 3 5 7 9 10 8 6 4 2

Library of Congress Cataloging-in-Publication Data
Middleton, Charlotte.
Enrico starts school / Charlotte Middleton.
p. cm.
Summary: Enrico the cat starts school, but at
first he doesn't know how to make friends.
ISBN 0-8037-3017-9
[1. Cats—Fiction. 2. First day of school—Fiction.
3. Friendship—Fiction.] I. Title.
PZ7.M5845En 2004
[E]—dc22
2003016555

Enrico
Starts School

Charlotte Middleton

Dial Books for Young Readers New York

When he was four, Enrico was **great** at riding his bike.

Chico (Enrico's little brother)

training wheels

He was **awfully good** at sneaking up on his wind-up mouse. And he could make a **magnificent** sardine in lobster-jelly sandwich.

Now that he was **five**, Enrico was old enough for his first day at school.

funny new school shorts

The playground looked **awfully big**.

Enrico had **no idea** how to make friends.

In class he was **too shy** to put his paw up, even though he knew some of the answers.

At recess, Enrico tried to join some cats who were playing with their remote-control mouse . . .

cool mouse

but they were
not impressed
with his wind-up one.

At **lunchtime** Enrico sat with some other cats. He offered them a bite of his carefully prepared sardine in lobster-jelly sandwich . . .

but they showed **too much** interest in the sandwich . . .

empty tummy

empty lunchbox

and **not enough** interest in Enrico.

The other cats challenged Enrico
to **a race** at recess.

Enrico started the race **slowly**.

wobbly spools

But then his skates began to go *faster and faster . . .*

The roller skates hadn't been such a good idea after all.

But Chico had a new idea. He told Enrico to try just . . . being himself.

So, in the morning, Enrico set off for school with a **spring in his step.**

In class he put his paw up . . .
and got the answer **right!**

At recess
Enrico didn't
really mind
playing on
his own . . .

Enrico . . .
being himself

but he was **very pleased** when he felt a gentle tap on his shoulder.

A rather shy cat said his name was Pepe and asked if he could play with Enrico.

best
buddies

After school Enrico invited Pepe
to play at his house.

little chums

Chico was playing with a new friend too.
It was **Miguel**, Pepe's little brother.

Enrico, Pepe, Chico, and Miguel spent all afternoon making an exciting course for Enrico's model train set . . .

and Enrico's sardine in lobster-jelly sandwiches were the **most** **magnificent** he had **ever** made.